Dear Parent:
Your child's love of reading starts here!

Every child learns to read in a different way and at his or her own speed. Some go back and forth between reading levels and read favorite books again and again. Others read through each level in order. You can help your young reader improve and become more confident by encouraging his or her own interests and abilities. From books your child reads with you to the first books he or she reads alone, there are I Can Read Books for every stage of reading:

SHARED READING
Basic language, word repetition, and whimsical illustrations, ideal for sharing with your emergent reader

BEGINNING READING
Short sentences, familiar words, and simple concepts for children eager to read on their own

READING WITH HELP
Engaging stories, longer sentences, and language play for developing readers

READING ALONE
Complex plots, challenging vocabulary, and high-interest topics for the independent reader

ADVANCED READING
Short paragraphs, chapters, and exciting themes for the perfect bridge to chapter books

I Can Read Books have introduced children to the joy of reading since 1957. Featuring award-winning authors and illustrators and a fabulous cast of beloved characters, I Can Read Books set the standard for beginning readers.

A lifetime of discovery begins with the magical words **"I Can Read!"**

Visit www.icanread.com for info...
on enriching your child's reading...

D0401421

I Can Read Book® is a trademark of HarperCollins Publishers.

Danny and the Dinosaur: School Days
Copyright © 2017 by Anti-Defamation League Foundation, The Authors Guild Foundation, ORT America, Inc., United Negro College Fund, Inc.
All rights reserved. Manufactured in the U.S.A.

ISBN 978-0-06-228162-3 (trade bdg.) — ISBN 978-0-06-228161-6 (pbk.)

Book design by Rick Farley
21 CW   15 14 13   ❖   First Edition

I Can Read!

BEGINNING 1 READING

Syd Hoff's

DANNY AND THE DINOSAUR

School Days

Written by Bruce Hale

Illustrated in the style of Syd Hoff by John Nez

HARPER

An Imprint of HarperCollinsPublishers

Why don't dinosaurs go to school?
the dinosaur asked himself.

He knew his friend Danny

liked school,

so one day he left the museum

to see what school was all about.

The dinosaur saw Danny
inside a yellow bus
and decided to follow it
to school.

It was a beautiful day for a walk.

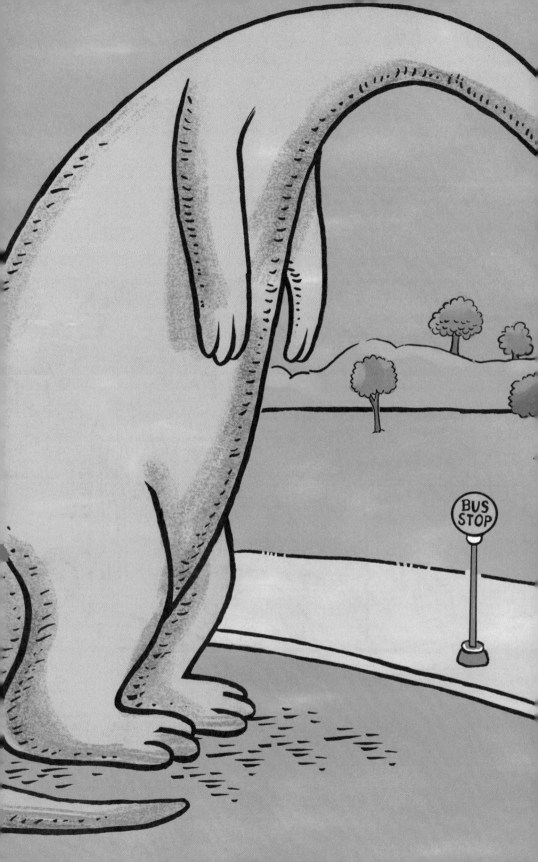

"What are you doing here?"
Danny asked the dinosaur.

9

"You made school sound like fun,"
said the dinosaur.

"So I wanted to come try it."

"Welcome!" said Danny's teacher.

It was a bit of a tight fit,
but the dinosaur joined
Danny's class.

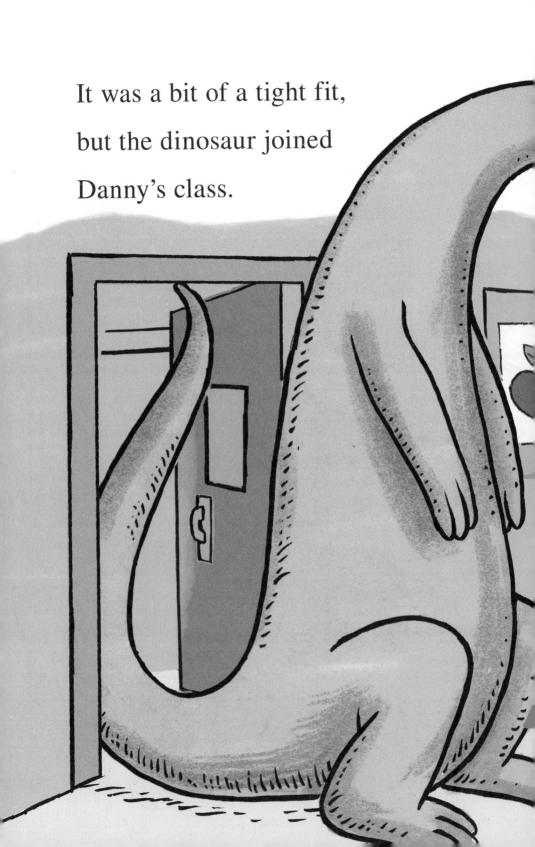

The dinosaur loved
learning his ABC's.

Danny's class learned
about math and measurements.

And the class learned what life was like one hundred million years ago.

The students made dinosaur art.

Danny's class even tried
stomping like dinosaurs!

After a busy morning of lessons,

everyone was hungry.

When the bell rang,

they raced out the door.

"Where's everyone going?"
asked the dinosaur.

"It's lunchtime," said Danny.

"Let's go eat!"

The cafeteria had sloppy joes.

"That's not dinosaur food,"

said the dinosaur.

Danny and the dinosaur got a pass
to go outside for lunchtime.

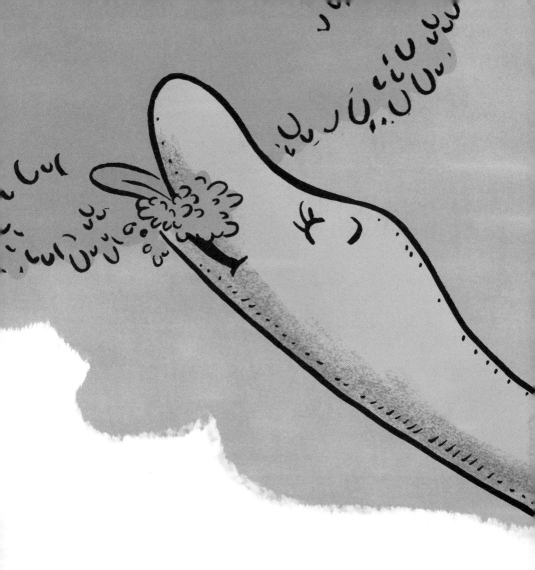

Danny ate his lunch,

and the dinosaur ate his!

It looked like so much fun,

the whole class joined them.

Everybody played on the grass.

"School is fun!" said the dinosaur.

"Yes, it is," said Danny's teacher.

"And so are you!"

Danny smiled.

"Our class has a present for you."

"Thanks!" said the dinosaur.

Everyone cheered.

Danny and his friends waved
as the dinosaur headed home.
"Come back anytime!"